Basil Hall Chamberlain, Eitaku

Urashima

Basil Hall Chamberlain, Eitaku

Urashima

ISBN/EAN: 9783744763202

Printed in Europe, USA, Canada, Australia, Japan

Cover: Foto ©Andreas Hilbeck / pixelio.de

More available books at **www.hansebooks.com**

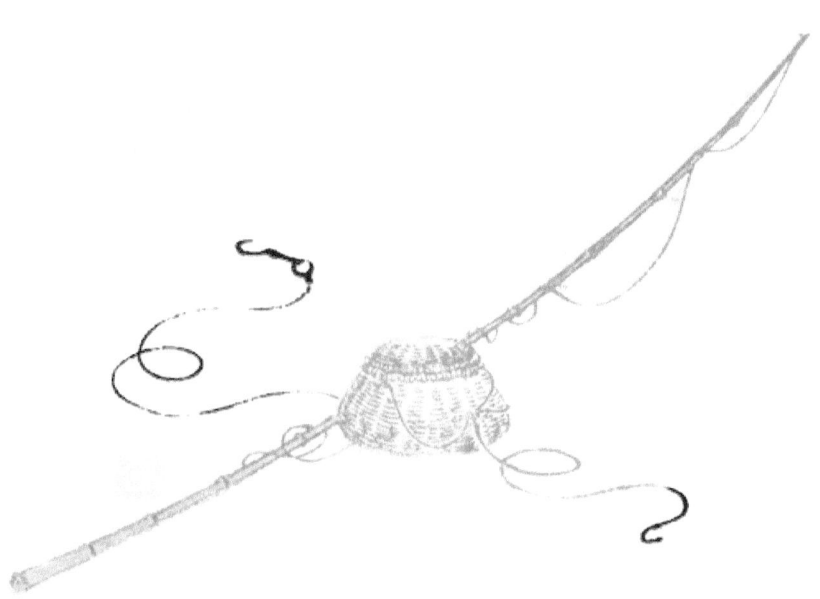

THE FISHER-BOY URASHIMA.

ong, long ago there lived
on the coast of the sea
of Japan a young fisherman
named Urashima, a kindly lad
and clever with his rod and line.

Well, one day he went out in his boat to fish. But instead of catching any fish, what do you think he caught? Why! a great big tortoise, with a hard shell and such a funny wrinkled old face and a tiny tail. Now I must tell you something which very likely you don't know; and that is that tortoises always live a thousand years,—at least Japanese tortoises do. So Urashima thought to himself: "A fish would do for my dinner just as well as this tortoise,—in fact better. Why should I go and kill the poor thing, and prevent it from enjoying itself for another nine hundred and ninety-nine years? No, no! I won't be so cruel. I am sure mother wouldn't like me to." And, with these words, he threw the tortoise back into the sea.

The next thing that happened was that Urashima went to sleep in his boat; for it was one of those hot summer days when almost everybody enjoys a nap

of an afternoon.   And as he slept,
there came up from
beneath the
waves a beauti-
ful girl,

who got into the boat and said:
"I am the daughter of the Sea-
God, and I live with my father
in the Dragon Palace beyond
the waves. It was not a tortoise
that you caught just now,

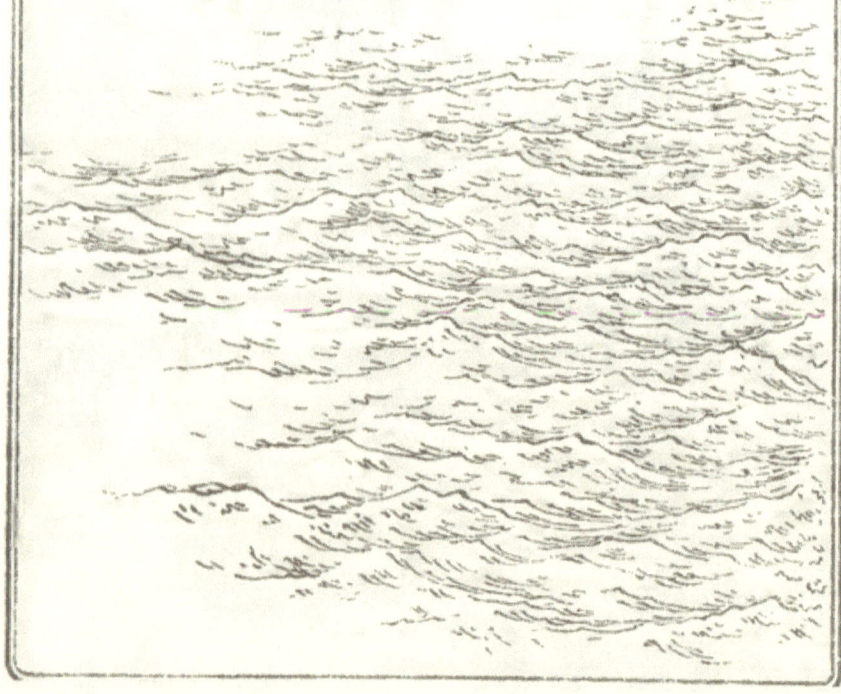

and so kindly threw back into the
water instead of killing it. It was
myself. My father the Sea-God
had sent me to see whether you
were good or bad.

We now know that you are a good, kind boy who doesn't like to do cruel things; and so I have come to fetch you. You shall marry me, if you like; and we will live happily together for a thousand years in the Dragon Palace beyond the deep blue sea."

So Urashima took one oar, and
the Sea-God's daughter took the
other; and they rowed, and they
rowed, and they rowed till at last
they came to the Dragon Palace
where the Sea-God lived and ruled
as King over all the dragons
and the tortoises and the fishes.

Oh dear! what a lovely place it was! The walls of the Palace were of coral, the trees had emeralds for leaves and rubies for berries, the fishes' scales were of silver, and the dragons' tails of solid gold. Just think of the very most beautiful, glittering things that you have ever seen, and put them all together,

and then you will know what
this Palace looked like. And
it all belonged to Urashima;

for was he not the son-in-law of
the Sea-God, the husband of the
lovely Dragon Princess?

Well, they lived on happily for three years, wandering about every day among the beautiful trees with emerald leaves and ruby berries. But one morning Urashima said to his wife: "I am very happy here. Still I want to go home and see my father and mother and brothers and sisters. Just let me go for a short time, and I'll soon be back again." "I don't like you to go," said she; "I am very much afraid that something dreadful will happen. However, if you will go, there is no help for it. Only you must take this box, and be very careful not to open it. If you open it, you will never be able to come back here."

So Urashima promised to take great care of the box, and not to open it on any account; and then, getting into his boat, he rowed off, and at last landed on the shore of his own country.

But what had happened while he had been away? Where had his father's cottage gone to? What had become of the village where he used to live? The mountains indeed were there as before; but the trees on them had been cut down. The little brook that ran close by his father's cottage was still running; but there were no women washing clothes in it any more. It seemed very strange that everything should have changed so much in three short years. So as two men chanced to pass along the beach, Urashima went up to them and said: "Can you tell me please where Urashima's cottage, that used to stand here, has been moved to?" — "Urashima?" said they; "why! it was four hundred years ago that he was drowned out fishing. His parents, and his brothers, and their grandchildren are all dead long ago. It is an old, old story.

How can you be so foolish as to ask after his cottage? It fell to pieces hundreds of years ago."

Then **it** suddenly flashed **across** Urashima's mind that the Sea-God's Palace beyond the **waves, with its** coral walls and its ruby fruits and its dragons **with** tails of solid **gold, must** be part of fairy-land, **and** that **one day** there **was** probably as long as a year **in** this world, **so that** his three years **in** the Sea-God's Palace **had** really been hundreds of years. **Of** course there **was** no use **in** staying at home, now that **all** his friends were **dead and buried,** and **even** the village had passed away. So Urashima was in a great hurry to get back to his wife, the Dragon Princess beyond the sea. But which was the way? He couldn't find it with no one to show it to him. "Perhaps," thought he "if I open the box which she gave me, I shall be able to find the way." So he disobeyed her orders not to open the box, — or perhaps he forgot them, foolish boy that he was. Anyhow he opened the box; and what do you think came out of it?

Nothing but a white cloud which floated away over the sea. Urashima shouted to the cloud to stop, rushed about and screamed with sorrow; for he remembered now what his wife had told him, and how, after opening the box, he should never be able to go to the Sea-God's Palace again. But soon he could neither run nor shout any more.

Suddenly
his hair
grew
as

white
as snow,
his face got
wrinkled,

and his back bent like that of a very old man. Then his breath stopped short, and he fell down dead on the beach.

Poor Urashima! He died because he had been foolish and disobedient. If only he had done as he was told, he might have lived another thousand years. Wouldn't you like to go and see the Dragon Palace beyond the waves, where the Sea-God lives and rules as King over the Dragons and the tortoises and the fishes, where the trees have

emeralds for leaves and rubies
for berries, where the fishes' tails
are of silver and the dragons'
tails all of solid gold?

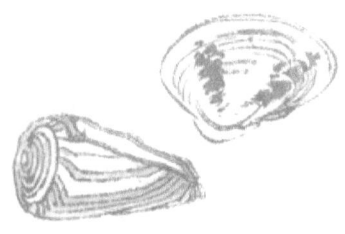